# The LITTLE PRINCE and the GREAT TREASURE HUNT

## by Peter Kavanagh

MACDONALD YOUNG BOOKS

Hi! I'm the Little Prince and this is my friend, Teddy.
We're visiting Uncle King John and Aunty Queen Mary.

for Sharon

Text and illustrations copyright © Peter Kavanagh

First published in Great Britain in 1996
by Macdonald Young Books
61 Western Road
Hove
East Sussex
BN3 1JD

Typeset in Poliphilus 18/25pt
Printed and bound in Belgium by Proost N.V.

British Library Cataloguing in Publication Data available.

ISBN: 0 7500 1880 1
ISBN: 0 7500 1881 X (pb)

What a dump this castle is! Not as good as our castle.

You're right, Little Prince.
Our castle is not as good as yours
it's much better!

Oh no, it's the Little Princess and her bear, Cuddly ⁄ they're girls.

I bet your silly old castle hasn't got moaning, groaning ghosts?

Yes it has.

I bet it hasn't got secret, creepy passages?

Yes it has.

I bet it hasn't got dark, gloomy dungeons?

Yes it has.

Well I bet it hasn't got hidden, buried treasure?

Er...no...it hasn't. Has yours?

Maybe it has and maybe it hasn't but I'm not showing you!

Quick, Teddy - after her!

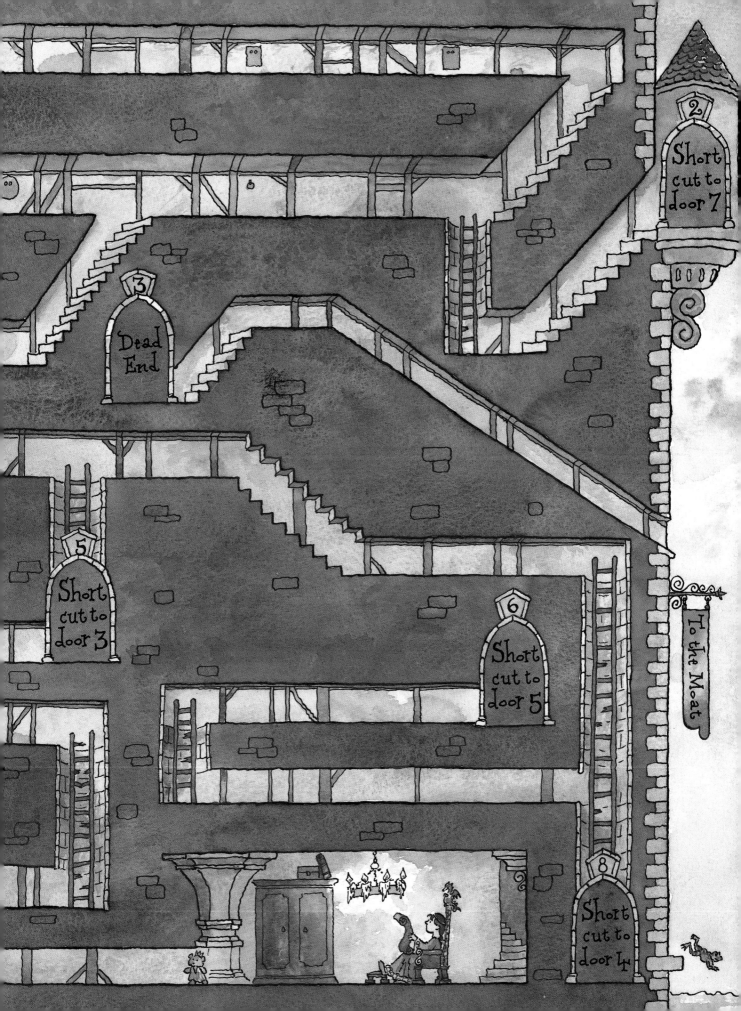

OK, Little Princess where is the buried treasure?
Are you sure you're brave enough to find out?
After all, you're only boys.

Teddy and I can face anything together. Can't we Teddy?

We will have to ask the Old Woman of the Wood. Read these rules and hope the wolf doesn't catch you!

# CRY WOLF

## A game to get you through the woods...

Play with two or more people using a die and counters. Take turns to move around the squares and follow any instructions you land on.

Anyone who throws a five becomes the wolf and chases everyone. If the wolf lands on your counter you're caught. Go to the wolf's den. Take your turn with the die but you cannot move until the wolf is caught. (Only one wolf at a time.)

The wolf is caught when anyone, except the wolf, throws a one. The wolf is now a player again and continues the game from the den.

The game is over when somebody reaches the Old Woman's cottage and the story can continue.

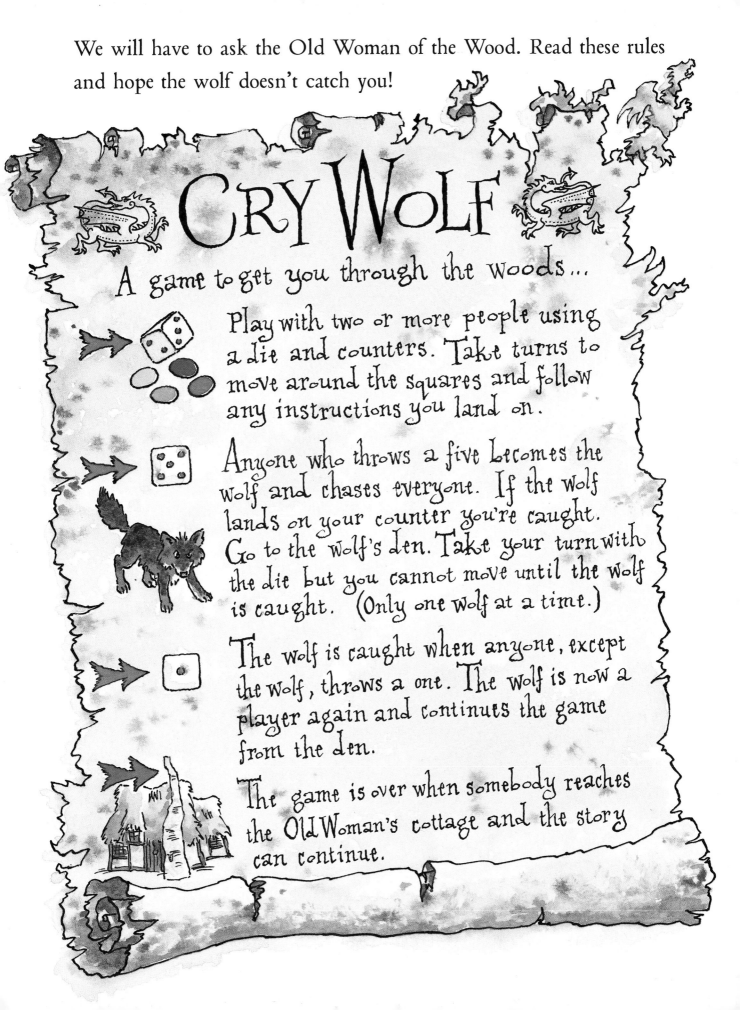

THROW 6 to START

FOLLOW ARROW

FOLLOW ARROW

FOLLOW ARROW

Hello, children,
have you come for tea?
You do look delicious...

No, Old Woman of the Wood. We've come to
ask you where we can find the treasure
hidden in King John's castle.

And what will you give me, children, in return for my answer?
Will you give me your teddy bears for my collection?

No, we love our teddies too much.
Come on Little Princess, let's go home.

Wait, children, you are right! A good teddy is worth
more than any hidden treasure.
But I cannot help you unless you bring back my five
golden rings from the Naiads in the lake.

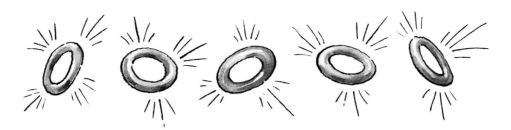

Can you swim, Little Prince?

Like a frog, Little Princess.

Now I can reach up to get you this key. You must seek the Laughing Doors in the castle. Beyond the door that this key opens, you will find the treasure hidden in a small, wooden chest.

Thank you, Old...er...Young Woman of the Wood.
OK, let's get back to the castle!

It's my castle so I get to open the chest.
OK, OK! What's inside?

It's a little, golden dragon...and it's alive!

And I fly Little Princess.
Am I not a wonderful treasure to have found?
But tell me this, is it not more wonderful
to have a treasure yet to find?

So follow me, back through the book
and hunt again for a dragon
hidden on every page.

Come on, everyone!
Back to the beginning!